Everlee, Love those crab cakes!

Love

Pat Goldy

Crab Cake Thanksgiving

Written by Pat Goldys

Illustrated by Marilyn Thomas Kadantot

Dedication

Dedicated to all my friends and family in Baltimore, Maryland.
They continue to enjoy steamed crabs, snowballs, candy and cake that are the best in Maryland.

Special thanks to my daughter in law, Michelle, who makes the best Thanksgiving meals in Florida for our family. One time we did have crab cakes and we didn't miss that turkey one bit!

Thanksgiving dinner, the best food event.

Turkey, veggies, potatoes and pies.

Mom is cooking family recipes.

Shopping for days to get all the supplies.

Get up early to start the cooking.

Aromas and smells wake the sleepy up.

Everyone but mom has something else to do.

And don't even touch a measuring cup.

Mom is the only chef

who does it all!

"Dinner's ready!" only

she would call!

The turkey goes in the oven.

The rolls are baking, broccoli steaming.

The sweet potatoes have marshmallows.

That delicious meal keeps us

daydreaming.

Who will help?

Uncle Matt, firefighter, hoses down fires!

Aunt Alicia takes Tofu for a stroll.

Dad gets bait and goes fishing

With Mila and her fishing pole!

Grandma and Pop sleep late.

They need their rest!

Uncle Mike surfs early

When waves are best!

Mom is chosen
To make this big meal.
She loves cooking.
It's no big deal!

She defrosts the giant turkey,
And notices an awful smell.
"Oh no! This turkey is bad!"
"What will we eat?" Mom did yell.

"The stores are closed!
No turkeys left to buy!
Must figure something out!
No time to cry!"

Mom searches the freezer,
Finds crab cakes in delight!
Maryland crab cakes are delicious!
Every single bite!

So, the delicacy is placed
on the huge oval turkey plate!
A new tradition is born today!
Wonder if the family will debate?

Next, Mom cuts the veggies—
carrots, potatoes, string beans!
Mom gets another idea!
She hopes it's not too extreme!

These veggies work best,
If put in crab soup.
Add some seasoning.
Now taste a little scoop.

Thanksgiving dinner can be,
Whatever you like to eat.
Every family likes different foods.
So make your meal unique!

Next Mom makes the appetizer.
More crab in place of turkey meat.
She rolls little balls of crab
For the great Thanksgiving feast!

Thanksgiving is a special time,
To share a meal with all you love.
It's about being with
Who you think the world of!

Crab balls are not enough.
A crab pretzel added to eat
Is just the right touch
To make the meal complete!

Hungry for a tasty dessert!

Need gooey, chewy sweets to eat.

Taffy, caramel creams, and cowtails,

Yummy Maryland candy treats!

Everyone gets thirsty.
What should we drink?
An old fashioned snowball!
That's what we think!

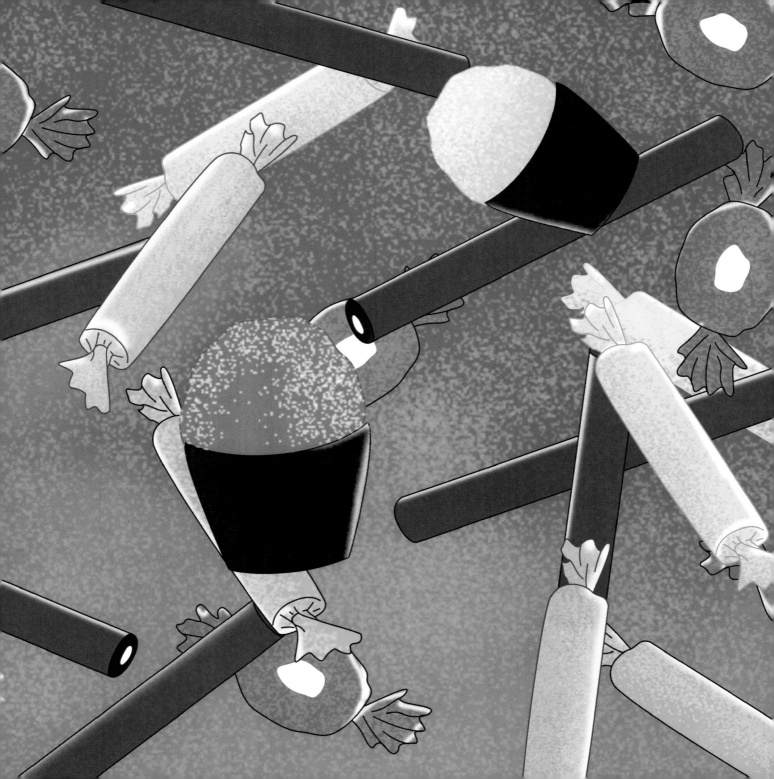

No leftovers to be seen!

Everything gobbled up! All gone!

This is the first Thanksgiving ever

Where it felt like something was kind of wrong!

We miss our turkey!
We love our crab cakes!
Is this a new tradition
Or a great big mistake?

The next day all were hungry.
No leftovers did we have to munch.
So Mom got a turkey.
A turkey for lunch!

This turkey had a different smell!
A whiff of seasoning
would reveal
This turkey was stuffed with crabmeat!
A new food tradition
after our Thanksgiving meal!

We give thanks for all the food.
No matter what we eat!

As long as no one goes hungry.
At our table,
there's always an extra seat!

CAN YOU FIND THE MARYLAND
SYMBOLS ON EACH PAGE?

Blue Crab

Chesapeake Bay Retriever

Black Eyed Susan

Baltimore Checkerspot Butterfly

White Oak Tree

Ecphora Shell

Diamondback Terrapin Turtle

Calico Cat

Smith Island Cake

Maryland Flag

CAN YOU FIND THE FLORIDA SYMBOLS
ON THE LAST PAGE?
Orange Tree
Fresh Orange Juice
Palm Tree
Florida Flag
Alligator
Manatee
Zebra Longwing Butterfly
Mockingbird
Orange Blossom Flower

Pat Goldys was an educator for 39 years in Baltimore, Maryland. She was a teacher, assistant principal, and principal. She is a mother of 3 grown sons and 2 daughters in law. She has one granddaughter, Mila, who inspires the many stories for the books!

Pat started her writing career at 64 years old and has many ideas for future children's books.

@AuthorPatGoldys

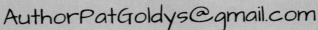
AuthorPatGoldys@gmail.com

If you choose to read, please leave a review as I'd love to read your thoughts!

Pat Goldys was born in Baltimore, Maryland and lived there for 63 years. She loves steamed crabs at Jimmy's Famous Seafood, Old Bay seasoning, Goetze's caramel creams, cow tales candy, Ocean City saltwater taffy and snowballs. She moved to Florida to be near her granddaughter, Mila. The pandemic came and Thanksgiving dinner was outside, which you can do in the warm Florida weather. This book is based on our second Thanksgiving in Florida.

It turned out great!

Made in the USA
Columbia, SC
24 September 2021